THE PLOT OF THE PERILOUS PIRATE

CAPTAIN SMITTY TAKES OCEAN CITY, MD

SO-ARK-852

MAINSTAY PUBLISHING

Denise Blum   Lisa Sanderson

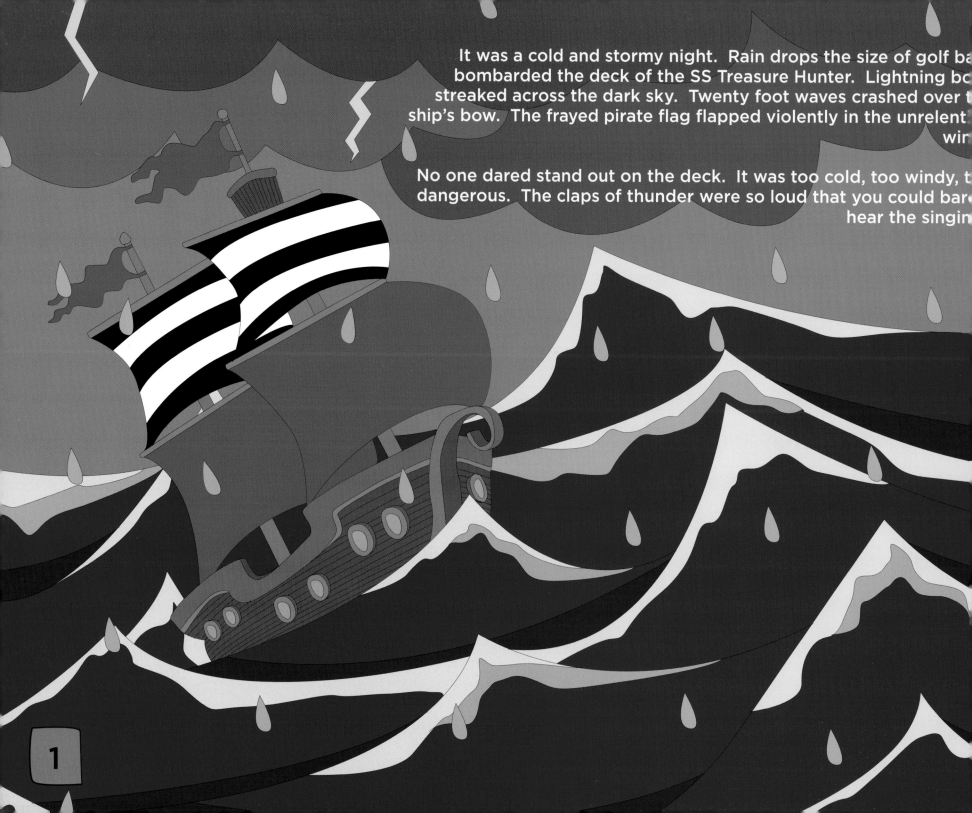

It was a cold and stormy night. Rain drops the size of golf ba[lls] bombarded the deck of the SS Treasure Hunter. Lightning bo[lts] streaked across the dark sky. Twenty foot waves crashed over t[he] ship's bow. The frayed pirate flag flapped violently in the unrelent[ing] win[d.]

No one dared stand out on the deck. It was too cold, too windy, t[oo] dangerous. The claps of thunder were so loud that you could bar[ely] hear the singin[g]

1

THE SINGING?!?

Down in the galley of that big old pirate ship, in the middle of one of the worst storms of the century, was a gathering of the craziest, quirkiest pirates around. There was Crabclaw Cassidy, Jellyfish Jane, Chargin' Chase, Battleship Bobby and Madcap Molly.

2

Then there was Pirate Smitty. Smitty was turning eight years old and having a birthday party. The galley was decorated with black balloons. The pirate partygoers ate cake iced with weevils and played pirate party games like Cannonball Catch and Pin the Tail on the Rat.

And there were presents. Lots and lots of presents... a shiny new hook, a purple eye patch, a golden peg leg.

Smitty's favorite present was a treasure map given to him by Pirate Pop, his grandfather.

Pop explained, "Argh! Some day when ye be older, ye will travel to far off distant lands. Exotic lands, filled with beauty and excitement. Paradise. And there ye will find treasure beyond yer wildest dreams."

"Shiver me timbers! What is this exotic land called?" Smitty asked. He couldn't wait to follow the treasure map!

"Ocean City," said his grandfather in a mysterious voice. "Ye won't find another place like it."

4

Through the years, Smitty often dreamed of Ocean City. Would he find gold? Jewels? A treasure chest full of money?

One day, while Smitty was polishing his compass, he felt a peck at his shoulder. It was Pop's parrot and she was carrying a note in her beak. Smitty opened the note and read it. The message simply said, "It is time."

Smitty knew immediately what that meant. It was time to go hunt for his treasure in Ocean City!

Smitty gathered his best pirate playmates - Crabclaw Cassidy, Chargin' Chase and Madcap Molly. They prepared the ship, grabbed Pop's parrot and set sail.

The crew rode out violent storms at sea, battled three headed sea monsters, and encountered sharks the size of whales! Yet they persevered. Nothing was going to stop them from getting to Ocean City!

Then finally, one day Smitty looked though his telescope and saw it...he couldn't believe his eyes. "Land Ho!" he bellowed. "Well at least me thinks it's land...what exactly IS that?"

6

The view through his telescope showed a land that looked, well, bizarre to him. He saw flashing lights and brightly colored thing-a-ma-bobs whirling through the air. As the ship drew closer to land, he heard pops and pangs and pings mixed with music and laughter. This was the strangest place he had ever visited! It was soooooo different from the pirate world he was used to.

Smitty and his mates anchored the ship, grabbed the treasure map and headed to shore.

The first stop on the map was the Ocean City Life-Saving Station Museum. "Me hearties, let's find our fortune!" Smitty ordered.

pirates began their treasure hunt. They analyzed artifacts, studied the surf boats and mulled over the Mermaid hibit.

itty investigated the Aquarium Room. As he checked the tanks, he spotted the blue crabs. Wanting to get a ser look, Smitty peered down into the tank, his face almost touching the water.

d idea. A crab reached up, pinched Smitty's nose and held on!

itty's mates tried to help, pulling and prying, heaving and hauling, but that b would not let go!

argin' Chase had an idea. He held some pepper ler Smitty's nose. The pepper made Smitty eze.

CHOOOOOOOOOOO!" The sneeze startled the b, forcing him to release his grip... FINALLY!

crab scuttled back to the aquarium room as itty ran the other direction.

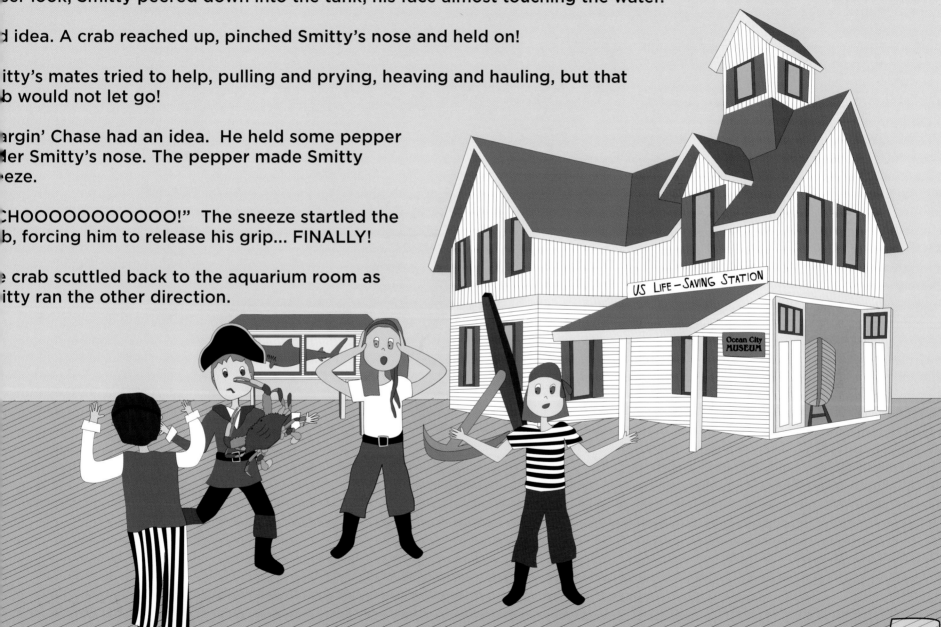

US LIFE-SAVING STATION

Ocean City
MUSEUM

8

Once he was rid of the blue crab, Smitty refocused his attention back to the treasure map. "Aye, mates. Looks like our next stop is the Park Place Hotel.

When Smitty looked up from his map, he saw Crabclaw Cassidy riding toward him on a four-wheeled bike. The didn't have anything like THAT back home.

"Smitty, jump in! 'Tis called a surrey. It be faster, and more fun, than walking," she exclaimed.

As the pirates pedaled to the hotel, they gazed at the sights around them... the boardwalk with its crowds of people and blinking lights, the beach with hundreds of brightly colored umbrellas. Ocean City was unlike anything the pirates had ever seen before! This was going to be an interesting adventure!

Park Place Hotel was buzzing with activity. There were vacationers swimming in the pool and sunbathing on deck. The clothing boutiques and jewelry store were packed with shoppers looking for souvenirs. Conner's ch Cafe was loaded with hungry customers snacking on sweet potato fries and fruit smoothies.

pirates inspected the hotel from top to bottom. They checked the hallways, the front desk and the restaurants.

itty searched the pool area. The sun was shining brightly and cast a sparkle on the surface of the ter. From a distance, it looked like the pool was filled with shiny gems. Smitty jumped into the ter, excited! He jumped out of the water, disappointed. It was just a reflection. No gems, no jewels. here would he find his treasure?!?

Next stop...The Dough Roller. The tables were filled with people eating pizza, pancakes and Italian dinners. Something shiny caught Smitty's attention. Could it be... silver? Here?!? (The silver was actually silverware...fork knives and spoons. But anything that shiny looked like treasure to Smitty!)

The pirates tried to seize the silverware. It wasn't easy. Those landlubbers protested! They hid their forks under napkins and covered their knives with menus.

Finally, a young boy put an end to the chaos. When Smitty tried to take his silverware, he speared Smitty in the hand with his fork!

Smitty pulled back his aching hand and looked up...he froze in his tracks. Everyone in the restaurant was holding fork and pointing it at him, ready to take action! "Mates, time to go... NOW!" he ordered.

11

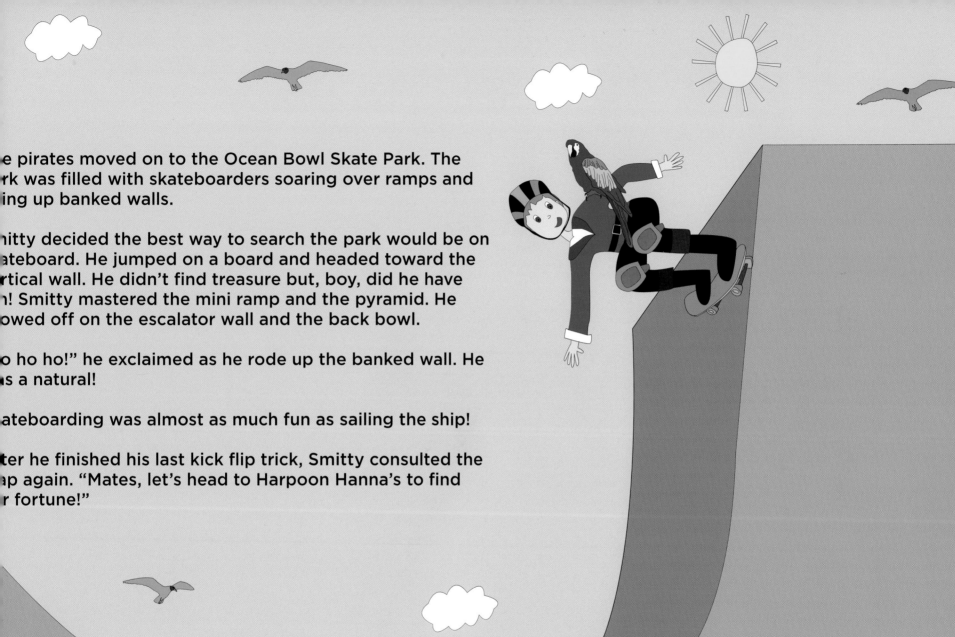

e pirates moved on to the Ocean Bowl Skate Park. The
rk was filled with skateboarders soaring over ramps and
ing up banked walls.

nitty decided the best way to search the park would be on
ateboard. He jumped on a board and headed toward the
rtical wall. He didn't find treasure but, boy, did he have
n! Smitty mastered the mini ramp and the pyramid. He
owed off on the escalator wall and the back bowl.

o ho ho!" he exclaimed as he rode up the banked wall. He
s a natural!

ateboarding was almost as much fun as sailing the ship!

ter he finished his last kick flip trick, Smitty consulted the
ap again. "Mates, let's head to Harpoon Hanna's to find
r fortune!"

12

As the pirates entered Harpoon Hanna's, the smell of fresh flounder and tasty tilapia filled the air. "Aye, smells like the ocean, mates. Treasure must be close!" Smitty remarked.

The pirates checked under oysters, and alongside the scallops. They dashed through the dining room and darted in between tables on the deck.

As Smitty passed the restaurant's waterfall, he noticed a mural painted on the wall behind it. The parrot in the mural looked like Pirate Pop's parrot. Was this a clue or just a coincidence?

Smitty had no time to ponder the possibilities. Customers were beginning to point their forks at him... oh no, not the forks again! THAT was definitely a clue... it was time to leave!

The map guided the pirates to the jetty, where landlubbers were fishing for flounder and trout. Smitty crossed his fingers, then cast his rod. He was fishing for pirate plunder and was hoping to pull up a chest stuffed with jewels... white diamonds, green emeralds, blue sapphires.

Instead, the closest Smitty came was pulling up a bluefish.

"Arrrrr!" he mumbled in frustration.

But Smitty was not giving up! Pirate Pop had told him many years ago that Ocean City held treasure beyond his wildest dreams. He was determined to find it! "Where to next, mates?" he asked.

"Hooper's Crab House, Smitty," said Crabclaw Cassidy. "Let's go!"

The pirates arrived at Hooper's Crab House tired and hungry. They had been treasure hunting all day and weren't having any luck. They decided to eat while studying the map. They gobbled up grouper, munched on mahi mahi and cracked open crabs.

Smitty gazed through the window as he ate. Something caught his eye... a boat named Pirate Pete's was tied to Hooper's dock. Could this be a clue to where the treasure was hidden? The pirates rushed outside and boarded the vessel.

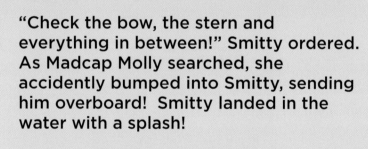

"Check the bow, the stern and everything in between!" Smitty ordered. As Madcap Molly searched, she accidently bumped into Smitty, sending him overboard! Smitty landed in the water with a splash!

"This is NOT going well," Smitty grumbled as he swam to shore.

...s Smitty's treasure at the playground?

...the pirates searched, they took over the entire play area. They turned over swings and blockaded slides. They
...en jammed up the monkey bars.

...e children at the playground were not happy and decided to take matters into their own hands. Smitty felt some-
...ng cold hit his foot. A little boy had dropped an ice cream cone on him!

...en he felt something cold on his other foot. A little girl had done the same thing! What was going on here?

...looked up and saw several other children, all holding ice cream cones, all pointing them at Smitty. "This is OUR
...yground," said the little girl. "Stop hogging it or face an ice cream shower!"

...e pirates ran as ice cream scoops started flying toward them!

The treasure map pointed them to Jolly Roger's Splash Mountain Water Park.

There were water slides and pools everywhere. "Me hearties, look under every raft. Search every pool!" ordered Smitty.

Chargin' Chase searched the Ragin' Rapids Ride. Crabclaw Cassidy jumped on The Cannonball Slides and Madcap Molly hunted for jewels in the Wave Pool.

Smitty spotted a giant pirate head on top of a tree house in the Rain Forest. He was sure this was a clue to finding his treasure. He maneuvered his way past slides, water wheels and tipping buckets. Something moving overhead caught his attention. He looked up just in time to see a tidal wave of water being dumped out of the pirate head... right on top of him!

17

ay, so maybe the giant pirate head wasn't a clue
er all... but Smitty wasn't discouraged. The next
ps on his map were Jolly Roger's Speedworld and
usement Park.

eedworld was filled with race cars zooming around
cks of all shapes and sizes. The pirates searched
de stockcarts, under supertrucks and behind
rmula One cars.

ey explored some of the Amusement Park rides...
Carousel, the Bumper Cars, the Teacups. Then,
itty spotted the Wacky Worm. Could this be where
treasure was hidden?

He climbed into the Worm. It barreled
down the track, twisting and turning at
high speeds. Smitty closed his eyes
and held on with all his might.

"AAAAAAAAHHHHHHHHHHH!" he
shrieked. When the ride finally
stopped, he stumbled off and fell to the
ground in relief.

Treasure hunting was wearing him out!

18

WELCOME TO HARBOR DAY!

The pirates headed to the docks of West Ocean City. There was a sign that rea "Welcome to Harbor Day!" As the pirates continued their quest, they saw landlubbers learning how to clean fish, harvest scallops and mend nets.

At last, the pirates felt like they fit in! An entire festival devoted to life at sea!

Smitty passed two boys talking about ocean safety. They called to Smitty. "Captain, you must face dangers at sea all the time. Can you give us some tips how to stay safe?"

Smitty thought for a moment. "Batten down the hatches, don't let rapscallions scuttle ye vessel and mind ye captain or face the keelhaul."

"Huh?" they muttered in confusion. Where was a Pirate-to-English dictionary when you needed one?

19

When the pirates arrived at Fishtales, treasure was on their minds.
"Me hearties, search for doubloons!" Smitty ordered.

They checked under chairs and turned over tables. They ransacked rockfish and pillaged pizza.
They didn't find treasure but, boy, did they make a mess!

Suddenly, Smitty felt something hard hit him in the head. He looked down and saw a pink sneaker.
He looked up and saw a one-sneakered girl glaring at him.

"That was MY pizza!" she bellowed. She was angry!

"Well that was MY head!" Smitty retorted.

"My brother's sneakers are MUCH BIGGER than mine,"
she warned.

Smitty looked at her brother's BIG feet, then made
a quick decision. "RETREAT!" he shouted as he
and his mates dashed to the exit. They
narrowly escaped as a second pink sneaker
came hurtling toward them.

20

Next stop... Assateague Island.

The pirates walked down the beach, digging holes in the sand and peeking under seaweed. They searched unde
trees and around sand dunes.

A herd of Assateague's famous wild ponies meandered onto the shoreline. Smitty was SURE they would lead hir
to the treasure. He followed them for a long while. No luck.

Smitty stopped to admire a bald eagle flying above him. He watched as it flew in circles, getting closer and clos
It seemed to be flying right at him!

The eagle landed on Smitty's head!

It only stayed a few moments, but that was long enough for it to leave a "present" on Smitty's hat. Yuck!

pirates headed to Wockenfuss Candies where they were greeted by the sweet smells of sweet treats.

the first time all day, treasure was not on Smitty's mind. He was hypnotized by the mountains of candy that rounded him. It had been a long hard afternoon. He deserved a little treat, didn't he?

reached into a bowl and began pulling out handfuls of super-sticky-oh-so-yummy taffy. It was delicious! Soon, itty's hands were so sticky he couldn't put the bowl down. It was stuck to him!

ates, help me!" he called. The pirates tugged and twisted, grabbed and grappled. After what seemed like an r, they finally pried the bowl off of him!

y left without treasure, but with armfuls of candy and big smiles on their faces.

Wockenfuss

22

The crew explored the miniature golf course. Smitty spotted a g
pirate ship in the middle of the course. He thought this MUST be a
to where the treasure was hidd

The pirates scoured the ship but found noth

Suddenly, a golf ball came soaring through the air and hit Smitty on
head! "Avast, we be under attack! Cannonballs be in the a

The pirates expected to hear a loud "boom" as the cannonball explod
Instead, all they heard was "Oo

Cannonballs don't say "Oo

A boy approached Smitty. "That's my golf ba
accidently hit it off the course." The boy picked up
ball and walked aw

"What's a golf ball?" Smitty wondered. Ocean
was so different from his pirate ho

OLD PRO GOLF

THE BUCANEER

...ow what?!?

The pirates had searched everywhere! They had followed the map all over Ocean City... but still, no treasure.

"Did we miss a clue somewhere? Did we overlook something?" Smitty wondered.

He studied the treasure map again. The parrot squawked in his ear.

Smitty froze. Then, slowly, a smile appeared on his face. He looked at the parrot. He hugged the parrot! Then he announced to his mates, "Avast! I know where the treasure be!"

The pirates looked at him expectantly.

"We missed the most important clue, mates. Something was pointing at the treasure and we missed it!" Smitty explained.

The pirates looked at him in confusion.

"The parrot! Pop's parrot brought me the note that started our journey. Pop's parrot will help us end the journey too!"

The pirates were STILL looking at him in confusion.

"Me hearties, the treasure is hidden at...

24

"HARPOON HANNA'S!"

They rushed back to Harpoon Hanna's. The pirates followed Smitty over to the wall mural they had seen earlier. He pointed to the parrot in the painting. "The parrot's tail points to the waterfall. That's where our treasure be hidden!"

At the bottom of the waterfall was a treasure chest! They opened the chest to find it filled with diamonds and rubies, gold and silver coins, and a note.

Smitty read the note. It said, "Treasure is more than gems and coins. The real treasure you found is Oce
City! It's a place like no other. Paradise."

25

Smitty smiled and put the note in his pocket.

itty and the pirates went back to the ship, grabbed some sand chairs and headed to the beach. They decided hang out in Ocean City for a while and enjoy their treasure!

To Chris, Chase & Cassidy - I love you more than mint chocolate chip ice cream!
To Mom - Thanks for always being there for me! - D.B.

Ty and Molly - you make the cutest pirates. Sean - thanks for always believing in me. Love you all!
To my father-in-law, Bob, you are Pirate Pop! XO - L.S.

To my family and friends- couldn't have done it without you! -M.W.

Special thanks to our editors: Chase, Ty, Cassidy and Molly. Your ideas and opinions helped to make this book better than ever!

Written by Denise Blum. Illustrated by Melissa Walters.

Printed in the USA.

Mainstay Publishing
P.O. Box 293
Middletown, DE 19709
(302) 223-6636
publisher@mainstaypublishing.com
www.mainstaypublishing.com

ISBN 978-0-9832901-1-7

Other books by Mainstay Publishing...
The Dubious Dolphin Dilemma, A Delaware Beach Mystery